WHAT SHE DON'T KNOW

SECRET LOVE SERIES BOOK 1

MIA BLACK

CHAPTER 1

Remi

"UGH," I mumbled. I was in bed and the sound of my alarm had just woken me up from my sleep. It felt like I'd only just managed to get to bed and there I was having to get out of it. I stretched out my arm to turn off the alarm and then rolled over to other side of the bed to snuggle up to Jackson. It was my normal routine and I was so used to it.

I turned over in the queen-sized bed and threw my arm out, hoping to land it on his chest. But he wasn't there. It was then that I started to really wake up and realized that he wasn't there because he hadn't been there in months. He was in my dreams but not there in person because we'd gone through a nasty break up a few months prior.

That wasn't the first time it happened, sadly. I sucked my teeth and started to put it out of my head. I wasn't about to start the day on such a rough note. I didn't need that kind of drama swirling around in my head that early. Jackson was the past now and no matter how much I may have wanted him around, I wasn't about to go down that path again, not with his arrogant self.

I sat up and looked around my large bedroom. I'd recently redecorated it because I wanted it to have a different feel. You know how it is when you go through a breakup. You want to change things around, whether it's your appearance or your surroundings. I'd known people who'd moved clear out of the state just to avoid their exes. I wasn't that person. I wasn't about to let Jackson move me out of Atlanta for no reason. I'd gotten new furniture and let my hair grow longer...that was about it.

I was thankful that I had money and could pretty much do what I wanted to. I'd had people come in and paint and got a new bedroom set with a large king-sized bed. I didn't want to sleep in the same bed that I used to share with Jackson but no matter how big or different the bed was, it was still just as lonely.

I climbed out of bed and walked over to my huge walk in closet. I opened the door and walked inside. From ceiling to floor, there were all of these beautiful things I owned; shoes, dresses, bags, etc. Some of them were things I bought but a lot of it was stuff that I'd made myself. Being a fashion designer and stylist had its benefits. I didn't have to spend a lot of money on clothes. I wore my own shit most of the time. I had my closet organized by color because it seemed to be the easiest way to find anything. Lately my eyes always wandered down to the darker colors.

I looked at myself in the floor length mirror that took up space in my closet. I was glad that despite my breakup, I still looked damn good. I was 5'5" tall with brown skin the color of dark rum. I had cat like hazel eyes and naturally long eyelashes and thick eyebrows that I kept done. I had naturally curly, soft, jet black hair that came down to my bra when I straightened it. I had two deep dimples in either cheek when I smiled.

No matter how much I went through, I made sure that I always worked out so my body was always in check. I had a flat stomach and thick thighs, and a fat ass. My looks had served me well in my line of work and because of my looks, I'd been hit on by a bunch of people, guys and girls.

I decided to wear a black suit with white pinstripes. I took it out of the closet and laid it on the bed. Ever since my breakup I noticed that I'd been wearing a lot of black and white, which was out of my usual trend. I loved wearing color. It wasn't intentional that I kept wearing the simpler colors. Nothing else in my closet seemed to jump out at me much. As my Aunt Chloe kept saying, I was in my 'mourning phase' which was a normal thing after a relationship ended.

I got in the shower and got out just in time to hear my cellphone ringing loudly. I didn't even have to go over to it. The ringtone let me know that it was my Aunt Chloe calling, no doubt to let me know that she was outside. She was always so damned punctual. I thought about texting her and telling her I'd be there soon but I knew that it would only take up more time. I got dressed, throwing on the suit and simple black heels and headed out of my apartment and downstairs.

Aunt Chloe was sitting outside of my building in a black Bentley. She had more than one car but usually drove this one during the week because, according to her, she didn't want to be flashy. I didn't know what wasn't flashy about a car that cost almost $200,000 dollars but that was for her to figure out, not me. She was coming to drive me to work. It was a kind of ritual of ours at least once a week.

I greeted my doorman, James, and headed outside. I threw my purse in the backseat and climbed in the front, snapping on my seatbelt.

"Good morning," I said to her.

"Morning Remi," Aunt Chloe said. She was thumbing through her phone, no doubt skimming over emails or something. She was always busy with work in some way or form.

"Sorry for being late," I said to her. She was already putting the car into drive. She waved her hand dismissively and lazily drove off.

My Aunt Chloe and I had a great relationship, but my life was a lot more complicated than most people would have imagined it to be.

You see, my Aunt Chloe wasn't my biological aunt. When I was younger, I was adopted by the Montell family. They were well off and rich and took great care of me. I didn't want for anything. I didn't find out that I was adopted until after my adopted parents died in a horrible car accident. My Aunt Chloe, my mother's sister, took me in and raised me.

My mother had a public relations firm that dealt with a decent number of clients in our home of Atlanta. When she passed away, my aunt took it over. She had never really been interested in the work but she took over the company and put her business degree to work, putting Montell Public Relations on the map and turned it from a small mom and pop company with just a few clients to a nationally recognized and sought after PR firm. I was 23 now but I'd pretty much grown up in that office and knew it like the back of my hand. I still worked in the same space as my aunt but she'd given me my own office to run my business out if. I was a fashion stylist and designer who was building a name for herself with the help of my aunt.

"I just got hired a new associate who's

bringing along one of those New York Giants players," I heard my aunt say. We drove towards the office building that the firm operated out of. Truthfully, I wasn't really paying much attention to what she was saying.

My mind slipped to Jackson and how he and I had broken up. It was especially annoying because everywhere I went, I saw his face. Jackson Lyles was one of the hottest up and coming actors in Hollywood. He'd recently landed a part in a remake of some 80s movie as the lead and was earning a reputation as a young playboy now that we'd broken up. I was hurt by it. I couldn't lie.

"Remi!" my aunt said loudly. She slapped me on the arm and snapped me from my thoughts.

"Yeah?" I said. "Sorry about that. I got caught up thinking about something," I said to her.

She frowned at me but didn't seem to be mad. "It's alright," she said to me. "I know you're going through a lot because of your breakup."

I didn't say anything. I just stared out the window.

"Keep your chin up dear," she said. "If there's anything I know, it's that men come a dime a dozen."

I loved my Aunt and she and I had some great times together. I was just a little girl when my parents died and she took me in. Most of my life I'd been raised by her. I was about 8 years old and she took me to her house and told me that I'd be staying with her from now on. She gave me my own bedroom and told me that whenever I was ready, she and I would talk about everything that was going on.

When I felt up to it, we spoke. She made it clear to me that she wasn't trying to replace my parents because no one could do that. She said that she didn't have any kids and didn't really want any but I was her niece and she'd love me like I was her own. I was appreciative of it. My aunt was still young at the time so I knew it was a lot for her to deal with but she did it. She made sure that I had everything I could ever want and need. I wasn't spoiled but she tried her hardest to provide me with the best that she could while still working on the company. She'd worked hard to raise me in her image and I was the woman I am now because of her.

I loved Aunt Chloe but I also kept her at a distance. When I was younger, my mother told me that Chloe was a lot to deal with. When I asked her what she meant she clarified. "Sweetheart, I love your aunt and you should too, but behind all the flashiness of the life she lives, she can be a dark person. Never forget that," my mother said to me one day. Over the years, I'd seen Aunt Chloe get damn near ruthless when it came to other people, but she'd never done that to me. We'd never had any real issues though. I hoped that it never came down to it between she and I.

"Remember that my gala is in a few days," she said to me. "You have to be there."

"Of course," I said. "I wouldn't miss it for the world." When I was younger, I loved the gala events that my aunt threw. I was always excited to see all of the celebrities and entertainers but now that I was older, they started to become a little boring. I was going to go through and support. Plus, it wouldn't look right if I wasn't there.

We got to the office and my aunt arrived and handed her keys to the parking garage attendant to park her car. The parking attendant, Charlie, looked her up and down, staring at her frame.

Aunt Chloe was a beautiful woman. She was only 40 years old but she didn't look anywhere close to her actual age. She was 5'6" with mocha latte colored skin. She had these gorgeous slanted brown eyes that complimented her signature haircut: a pixie cut that had been dyed burgundy. She was like me when it came to working out but she went even harder than I did. She worked out with a personal trainer three times a week and made sure that she ate as healthy as possible. She had curves for days. Because of her beauty and the power she had from the line of work she was in, she always had a few men in circulation. She never really took anyone she was dating serious but she'd recently told me that she had a new boo and she'd be meeting him at the gala in a few days.

We both got on the elevator and I got off on the floor before she did and told her I'd see her later.

My aunt had given me a huge office space to use as my own. She supported me in my fashion styling and design career. Over the years, she'd sent a lot of clients my way; actors, singers, athletes, and more. I had a women's fashion line but I styled men and women. I was gaining a name for myself in the industry and I couldn't be happier about it.

I walked into my office and was immediately ambushed by Karla.

Karla was my best friend and assistant. I'd hired her because she was out of work and it just felt right to give her a job so that I could have her closer to me. Karla and I were really different at times.

First off, my girl was gorgeous. She could have been a model. She was 6'1" with this beautiful dark chocolate skin and these long, shapely legs that seemed to go on forever. She had a beautiful face and was curved in the right places.

She and I had been friends for years and she'd helped me out a lot in a bunch of situations. Karla was my girl and supported me in everything I did, even if it wasn't the right thing to do. She said that I needed to learn by experience.

"Morning!" Karla said brightly. She was smiling at me.

"Morning," I said to her as I walked over to my desk.

"Uh uh," Karla said. She screwed her face up at me as she looked me up and down. "You doing it again."

"What?" I asked. I sat down behind my desk and turned on my computer. I wasn't in a bad mood but I wasn't trying to get into whatever craziness Karla was about to try and tell me about myself.

"You come in here day after day in all these dark clothes and moping around here like you're at a funeral," she said. She walked over to me and sat at the chair in front of my desk. "I know that you and Jackson were together for a long time but it's time to move on. He moved on. We see that shit on the blogs," she said.

What she was saying was true. Being that Jackson was such a notorious person, it was no surprise that whatever he did ended up online. I used to get alerts every time something came up about him in the media but since we broke up I turned them off. The trouble was that with all of these Instagram blogs and stuff, Jackson was still a mainstay on my timeline at times.

"I know I'm not at a funeral," I said to her. I

leaned back in my chair. I knew that she wasn't going to drop it and that she did have my best interest in mind but damn if I felt like sitting there and talking with her. "I'm not even thinking about Jackson anymore." I was lying. She knew I was lying. A moment of silence passed between us.

She sighed loudly and kept going on. "Mmhmm," she said to me and rolled her eyes. "So I was thinking we should go out tonight," she said to me.

I shook my head. I hadn't been to a club in forever. They just weren't my thing. I guess that growing up privileged kind of made feel like I had to have other ways to have fun. "Nope," I said to her. "You know that's not my kind of thing."

"But it is mine," she said. She was persistent and I knew Karla wasn't about to drop it.

"Exactly why I'm not going," I said to her. "I ain't trying to be in some ghetto ass club, sweating my hair out and stuff."

She waved her hand at me dismissively. "Oh girl please," she said. "This is Atlanta." She raised her hands in a grand way like she was showing me something. "There are hot, sweaty ass clubs and there are nicer places we could go too. You acting like we haven't been friends for years. I know what type of shit you like."

I started to think about it. Maybe Karla was right. Maybe I did need to get back out into the world and see if there was a new man out there for me. "I guess we could go somewhere."

Karla burst out into a smile. "That's my girl. I got some places we can go. I'll see which places would be best for us."

The more I thought about it, the more excited I got. "I don't think I've been to a club since I turned 21, and that was two years ago."

"That's sad," Karla said. "It's alright though. Tonight, we gonna fix all your problems and find you a new man."

"I ain't holding my breath for that," I said to her with a smile on my face.

CHAPTER 2

Kaiden

I WAS SITTING at the huge table in the board-room of my father's company. I'd been sitting at this table for years. When I was younger, my father would bring me here and I'd run around under the table, but as I got older and actually started getting into the business, I got a permanent seat at it.

Around the table were other board members. One of the executives from a lower floor was doing a presentation about how we'd recently had an increase in sales. My father, Jacob, was looking at the man intently but his face showed no emotion. That was typical of my father when it came to business. He said that when it came to business, it was best to show no emotion when it could be helped.

My father had started a tech company over twenty years ago, in the early 90's. A lot of people had looked at him funny because back then people didn't think that the world of computers or the internet would become what it was today. Now, he had a multi-million-dollar Fortune 500 company, Briggs Technological Industries. In addition to that, he had several other companies and him and my mother had raised myself, my brother, and my sister to want to be businessmen and women ourselves.

I planned on following in my father's footsteps. Maybe not exactly in the world of technology but I planned on making sure that the plans I had for the future were going to happen for real. I was CEO of my own small company and sat on the board of a lot of my father's other companies. My pops was glad that I was following behind him. Unlike my dumbass little brother, Brandon, I was concerned about my future.

Brandon was sitting next to me and it was clear that he would have much rather been anywhere else in the world. He was 4 years younger than me, 21, but my father kept telling him that he wasn't a child and needed to make sure he was trying to make something for himself. He was good at hiding shit from our parents but not from me. I loved my brother dearly but he could be a fuck up and if there was anything he loved more than partying, it was women and pussy.

That was why it was no surprise when I looked over to him and though he was sitting up straight, he was smirking to himself. His eyes were looking down at his phone and he was texting someone. I could see the naked pictures in the text thread. I shook my head. I looked up and saw that my pops hadn't noticed anything.

I reached my hand over and grabbed the phone from him. He tried to hold on to it but when I subtly pointed over to my father, he let the phone go. I locked it and put it in my pocket.

"What the fuck?" he mouthed silently. He knew better than to say that shit louder than a whisper.

"We're in a meeting," I said. I had to lean over and whisper it to him so that no one else could hear or notice that we were talking. "You know that if pops sees you, that's your ass," I added in a voice so low only he could hear.

Brandon rolled his eyes and leaned back in his chair dramatically. Twenty minutes later the meeting ended and he and I got up and left the large office. We both walked into my corner office that looked out over the city of Atlanta. I handed him his phone back.

"You lucky I ain't tell pops about that shit," I said to him as I sat at my desk. He took a seat in front of it and immediately started going through the phone, no doubt texting whoever had sent him the nudes.

"Oh please," he said. "You his bitch, not me. I ain't scared of him. Besides, what he gonna say to me? 'Oh my son got some pictures of some bad bitches on his phone?'"

"Yeah, whatever," I said to him. Brandon stayed trying to tease me about working so hard for our father but it was what I wanted to do. I crumpled up a piece of paper from my desk and threw it at Brandon, hitting him in the forehead. "And that's for calling me his bitch." I smiled at him. My brother knew how to work my nerves but he was still my brother.

"Oh look, Kaiden the tough guy," he teased me.

"You should save your sexting for home. We work when we're here," I said to him. "Besides, you know what happened to me when pops caught me on my phone with some chick when I was supposed to be paying attention in a meeting before. I don't want you to go through that."

Brandon smiled. "Yeah, his ass was pissed off with you," he said to me. "He got over it though."

I shook my head. Brandon clearly wasn't trying to learn a lesson and I wasn't about to try and lecture him.

"Besides that," Brandon began, "you sexting days are over now. You got your old lady and shit like that."

"Shut up," I said to him.

"I mean, she's pretty and all she does have a bangin' ass body but she's a little too old for you," he went on. "At least in my opinion."

"Show some respect," I said. I was getting a little annoyed with him. "I didn't talk about none of those hoes you used to be sneaking in and out of your room when you lived at home and who knows what kinds of tramps you be bringing to your spot since you live alone now." I sat back in the chair and smirked. Brandon had always been low key sensitive in regards to us always teasing him about his choice of women.

"Oh please, ain't none of them my girl-friend. They're just that. Hoes." He paused, looking at the expression on my face and probably seeing that I wasn't in the mood for him or his shit. "I'm just teasing," he said. "Look, why don't you come out with me tonight?"

"I don't know about it," I said. "I got a lot of work to do and shit."

He sucked his teeth. "Oh please," he said. "Work can always get done. But you and I haven't been out in a minute. There's an event tonight that you'd like."

"What kind?" I asked. He was right. I hadn't been out to a party for a while. Because she was older, my new boo thought that a candlelight dinner was going out. I was only 25. I was in my prime and though I could be chill sometimes, I also wanted to get out and hear some music and shit too.

"That actor, Jackson something is in town

and is hosting a party at this lounge," Brandon said to me. "It ain't gonna be the typical Atlanta birds. Its industry people and people with money. Invite only."

I nodded my head in approval. It sounded like it could be fun but I wasn't lying when I said I had a lot of work to do around the office.

'I don't know," I said to him.

"Nah, you coming," he said to me. "You know we have a good time every time we go out, plus we ain't hang out in a while."

"Yeah, that is true," I said. "Man, remember when we went to Dominican Republic last year for your 21st birthday?"

"Hell yeah," he said. "I thought for sure one of us was gonna catch something, the way we were running through them chicks."

"Hell yeah," I said. That was the reason why I never judged Brandon too harshly. I was a lot like him when I was younger, just not as reckless. I did have my own way with women. They flocked to me and over the years I'd developed quite a reputation as a playboy. It helped that I had money but even before they knew that, my looks were more than enough to pull them in to me.

I was 6'2" with clear, golden brown skin. I had my mother's dark brown hair and I kept it styled in a short s-curl style and always had a fresh line up. I'd always been told I had a beautiful smile with bright white teeth, and my one dimple didn't hurt either. I worked out a lot and was built like a basketball player, slim but muscular at the same time. I made sure that I worked out often. Since I was young I'd always been a runner. My mother still had all of my track team trophies from when I was growing up.

"You were worse than me though," I said to Brandon. "You were doing too much. You gotta learn to slow down. Your dick gonna fall off or something." We both burst out laughing.

"Please," he said. "I'll be fine. You the one that's only 25 and trying to commit and shit. You need to come out with me tonight. I ain't gonna try and tell you to get wit' nobody. Just get out and see the world and all the beautiful women before you turn into pops."

I thought for a minute about how much I would enjoy myself. Brandon was right, honestly. There would always be time for me to do more work. I wanted to go out and enjoy myself and remember what it was like to be young. I didn't want to turn into my father before I had to.

"OK," I said to him. "I'm down."

"Great," he said with a smile. "It's gonna be a movie!" He was clearly excited and so was I.

CHAPTER 3

Remi

WORK WENT by quicker than I expected. I was busy as hell. People always needed to be styled for something and the more that my name got out there, the more they called me. I had Karla on the phone with a couple of boutiques all day and they sent over samples of things I'd need for clients. Being a celebrity stylist came with its own set of perks though. I wasn't really in the spotlight but had access to all the people who were. It was good and allowed me to make a lot of connections. Because of that, I had a lot of friends in the industry. I still wanted to branch out more and get a name for myself instead of as my aunt's niece

After work, Karla came back to my house. She was still on a high because I told her I'd go out with her. She'd run home during her lunch break and brought her clothes back. Once we got back to my apartment, she changed her clothes and was now in my closet looking for something for me to wear.

I loved Karla dearly and usually she was on point when it came to what she was wearing, but that night, it was just off. She was wearing this tiny ass sparkling black and white dress. Now, don't get me wrong, the dress itself was nice, but you have to understand that Karla was tall as hell. The dress wasn't the right fit for her and it ain't leave much to the imagination either. Karla had a nice body, but she could have picked something different, but I wasn't about to bring it up to her though.

"What are you looking for?" I asked her. I'd been sitting on my bed drinking a glass of wine and looking at her move from one side of the closet to the other. She was on a mission and I wasn't about to try and get involved. She'd insisted on helping me pick out something so it was on her to find it...whatever it was.

"I told you," she said, "I'm trying to find something for you to wear out tonight. You ain't been out in a while. You'd pick out the wrong thing."

I sighed and rolled my eyes. "Girl, you know I'm in fashion, right?" I asked her.

She stopped and turned to me all dramatic. "Duh, I work for you, don't I?" She was looking at me like I was a kid she was trying to help out. "I just want to make sure you have something that sends the right statement."

"And what statement is that?" I asked.

"Girl, that you're single, ready to mingle, and fuck anybody whose name happened to be Jackson," she said with a smile. I laughed at her craziness.

"I guess," I said, still laughing. "I just don't need my clothes making the same statements that your outfits say sometimes."

She stopped and turned to look at me. "And what's that supposed to mean?"

"I plead the fifth," I said with a slick smile.

After a couple more minutes, she came out of

the closet holding this red dress I hadn't seen in a while. Truthfully, I'd forgotten I had it. It was a red lace dress with long sleeves and entirely too short. It only came down to around my mid-thigh area. Most of the clothes in my closet were things I made, but that dress was a gift from a client.

"No," I said to her before she could even hand the dress to me. She walked over to me from the closet and handed it to me.

"Don't say no. You ain't even try it yet," she said to me.

"I don't have to," I said. "It doesn't fit right and it's not even my style. You know I don't usually wear anything like that."

"Girl, just give me a chance," she said to me. "Do I eve steer you wrong?"

I opened my mouth to answer and she beat me to the punch. "Ok, yeah, there have been a few times but just trust me. Go try the dress on. I know it's not your usual style but I want you to feel good about yourself. You gotta get back out there and see what the world is like."

I sighed. "Ok," I said, finally giving in. "I'll go try it on. But if I don't like it then I'm not wearing it."

"You're gonna like it," Karla said with a smirk.

I went into the bathroom and changed into the dress. Just as I predicted, it was short, much shorter than I thought it would be. It was also a lot tighter too. It was damn near a size too small. I walked back out and stood in front of Karla, holding my arms up to show her what it looked like

"Don't show it to me," she said. "You look good. Look at yourself in the mirror."

I walked over to the big mirror in the closet and took a look at myself. Damn, I really was feeling the dress. As much as I felt like it was too small or too tight, it didn't look like it at all. The red lace dress hugged my curves. I turned to the side and was happy to see my ass was looking really nice in it. I stretched out my arms, glad that I could actually move around in it.

"So what do you think?" Karla asked. She was smiling and I could tell by the look on her face that she already knew that I liked the dress.

"I like it," I told her. She started clapping like she was on a gameshow.

"Yes girl, you gonna be sexy as hell tonight,"

she said to me. "Now, I don't think you should wear any panties."

"Bitch what?" I turned around to face her. "Hell no."

"Girl, I can see your panties in this dress," she said to me. "You ain't trying to be at the club and have people looking at you cause of that all night, right?"

I loved Karla but she could also be embarrassing at times. I wasn't about to leave the house without any panties on. That was out of the question for real. "Not a chance," I said to her.

"You'll feel sexier if you don't wear any panties," Karla said. "Just give it a try."

I sighed. I didn't know what it was but after a little more thought I decided to just go with the flow. I hadn't been out in a while and I wasn't trying to act like a prude or anything. I slipped out of my thong and felt...different. I couldn't describe the feeling but between the glass of wine and the lace rubbing against my body, I knew that Karla was right. I felt sexier.

"Hmm," was all I said.

Karla knew me well and knew that I was

feeling it. "See?" She smirked at me. "Now, let's have another glass of wine and head out."

We headed out into my spacious living room where I put on some music. We poured out another glass of wine and we headed out. I wasn't the biggest drinker in the world so the two glasses of wine had me a little buzzed. We got an Uber and headed to the club.

We got out outside of the place where there was a line of people trying to get in. I also saw a bunch of girls in tight, brightly colored dresses. I had no doubt that they were trying to get inside too by using their looks. I would never want to put myself in that position. Karla and I walked up to the bouncer and he asked us for our names.

"We're under the name Remi Montell," Karla said. I side eyed her. I didn't know she'd used my name to get us on the list for this party. She should have told me.

"Come on in ladies," said the bouncer. We got inside of the huge club. It wasn't as packed as I expected it to be. There were a couple of VIP sections, some of which were occupied. I looked around as we waked in, spotting a couple of celebrities. I knew some of them and they waved as they saw me. I waved back as Karla and I walked over to the bar. The bar was clear across the room. The DJ was playing the music loudly and I was feeling it.

"What you wanna drink?" she asked me just as we got to the bar.

"Hmm," I said out loud. "Just get me whatever you're having."

"Ok cool," Karla said. "Can I get two whiskey and ginger ales?" Karla leaned over the bar, pressing her breasts up to try and get the attention of the cute bartender. He walked over and took her drink order and came back over with them a minute later.

She handed me mine and I took a sip. It was strong as hell, much more strong that what I was used to. I didn't really do dark liquor too often so it took me a few sips before I got used to the taste of it.

Karla and I spent the next hour or so on the dance floor. The celebrity DJ that they had was playing all the latest songs. I was hype as hell. Karla had danced with a couple of guys and she'd even convinced me to get with one or two of them.

"Girl, I'm glad you're getting out of your

shell," Karla said to me with a smile as we walked out of the bathroom and headed back to the dance floor. She wanted to touch up her make up.

We headed back out to the bar when the DJ came over the microphone.

"Now ladies and gentlemen, we have our celebrity host for the night! You all may have seen him in some of your favorite TV shows, but now he's making his transition to movies. Give it up for Jackson Lyles!"

The spotlights panned over to Jackson, who walked up to the DJ booth. He was smiling & holding the mic in his hands. He shook the DJ's hand and then looked out into the crowd. I overheard a bunch of women talking about how fine he was and stuff.

Jackson was a handsome man. I could never take that away from him. He was well over 6 feet tall and had mocha colored skin. He worked out regularly and had a nice body. He was on stage dressed in a pair of light blue jeans with a long white t-shirt. It fit his body and you could see the outline of his muscles. He was smiling as he looked at everybody and then I felt his eyes on me. Our eyes met and I felt a knot in my stomach.

"What the fuck?" I said out loud. Jackson was now talking to the crowd, getting them hype and stuff but I wasn't paying it any attention. I turned to Karla who looked just as shook as I did.

"Girl, I'm sorry," she said to me loudly over the music that was now playing again. "If I'd have known he was going to be here, I wouldn't have suggested that we come here. We can go if you want."

I'd be lying if I said the thought of getting up and leaving hadn't crossed my mind. Jackson had spotted me and I knew that he was going to try and piss me off. I didn't want to give him the opportunity of knowing he'd made me mad.

"Nah," I said to her. I shook my head. "No, it's fine. Let's just stay and have a good time."

We got back to partying and I made it a mission to ignore Jackson. That became much more difficult to do because he was the host for the night. He was putting on a show. He was throwing dollar bills at some of the dancers in the club and had the bottle girls bringing over what seemed like an endless number of bottles to him and the people in his section. Flashy motherfucker.

"Look," Karla said as we took a break from dancing, "I know you see Jackson doing shit. You know his ass is doing it on purpose to piss you off. You know what you need to do, right?"

"What?" I asked. It was like Jackson and I were playing a game. We hadn't looked directly at one another since he noticed me from the stage but I could feel his eyes on me. I also made sure never to get caught looking at him but he knew I had to be looking.

"You need to find someone to dance with and have some of your own fun," she said to me. "You need to find someone and just lay it on them. That'd make Jackson sick."

"I don't wanna play his game," I said to her. I did want to make him jealous but I didn't want to stoop to his level.

"It's not about trying to play his game. It's about having fun and showing his ass that you are ready to move on," Karla said. She began looking around like she was looking for someone and then she stopped moving.

"Look," she said, pointing to the other end of the bar, "down there. Those two are good looking and they're staring in our direction. And since there's two of them, we don't have to compete."

I turned my head and spotted the two guys she was pointing at. They were staring us down and didn't seem to have any problem with it. When they noticed us looking, one of them waved. They looked like brothers or something. They looked like one another. Before I knew what was going on, Karla had grabbed me by the arm and was walking us over to them. I didn't try and resist. The guys looked good.

We got over to them and in person they were much more handsome than I'd initially thought. They were almost the same height but one of them was just a little bit taller than the other. He also looked a little older too while the other one had a baby face.

"Wassup?" said the baby faced one. "I'm Brandon and this my brother Kaiden."

"Hey," Karla said. She smiled at them. They each shook their hands but I felt like a piece of meat because they were both looking me up and down.

"Nice to meet you," Kaiden said. He took my hand and shook it slowly, trying not to let it go. I almost didn't want him to. Even though he and his brother looked just alike, there was something I liked about him more.

"What brings you ladies in here?" Brandon asked. He was staring at my breasts. I felt self-conscious for a moment but I realized he was just attracted to me.

"I was trying to get my friend here to go out so she can enjoy herself," Karla said. I could hear tension in her voice. If I didn't know any better, I'd have assumed that she was jealous because they were paying me more attention.

"Cool, cool," Kaiden said. He hadn't really taken his eyes off of me. "Can we buy you ladies a drink?"

"Sure," I said with a smile. They got the attention of the bartender and ordered a round of drinks. I sipped on mine, another whiskey and ginger ale. I wasn't about to try and mix darks and lights.

We stood by the bar. It seemed like Brandon and Karla seemed to be making small talk, though I could feel him still making glances in my direction. Kaiden and I started talking over the music.

"So where you from?" he asked me.

"Here," I said. "Atlanta, born and raised. What about you?"

"Me too," he said. He smiled at me, showing all of his beautiful, white teeth. "So what brought you out tonight? Why was your friend trying to get you out the house tonight?"

I leaned back against the bar, feeling the alcohol taking over. I felt more relaxed. "Well, a couple of weeks ago I went through a breakup and she just wanted to get me out of the house."

"A breakup, huh? Somebody let you get away?" He looked me up and down again seductively and took a step towards me. The people closest to us got out of their chairs and we sat down in them. We were a lot closer now. Kaiden leaned into me and I could feel his warm breath on my face. "You look good," he said to me flirtatiously.

"Thanks. You do too," I said to him. "So what brought you out tonight?"

He was staring at my body and then looked up at me. "My brother dragged me out the house. If it were up to me, I'd be in the house or at the office taking care of some work."

"Me too," I said. "Looks like we have that in

common." I took a sip of my drink. The more I sipped, the better it tasted.

"Yeah, definitely," he said. "So tell me, why'd you and your ex break up? I mean...I don't know you too well but you seem like a quality chick. Plus, you're gorgeous."

I couldn't help but blush but I maintained my composure. "Just a bunch of stupid shit. I don't want to talk about it though," I said with a smile. I leaned into him a little bit more. "How about we just focus on what's here and now."

"I'm all for the here and now," Kaiden said as he licked his full lips seductively. He seemed so confident and sure of himself. It was such a turn on. "So what's happening here and now?"

"Well," I said, beginning to get a little more flirtatious with him, "there's me, an attractive woman in a club, talking to you, a handsome guy. And we're drinking and I think we're flirting with each other."

Kaiden smiled at me. "Yeah, that's what we're doing. I'm enjoying it too."

"Me too," I said.

We kept talking back and forth and it turned even more flirtatious. Out the corner of my eyes I saw Jackson staring at me. He wasn't trying to hide it either. I couldn't exactly see his face because I didn't want to turn my head but I figured he was probably pissed off. I decided to take it to the next level.

"You wanna dance?" I asked Kaiden. I grabbed his hand and finished the rest of my drink. He smiled and finished his too.

Kaiden and I headed out to the dance floor and started to dance. He could move and so could I. Every move that I made, he matched. For the first few minutes of us dancing, I was throwing it back on him because I was trying to make Jackson jealous. He was still staring at us, just not as openly anymore. The more I kept dancing though, the more I felt myself getting turned on by Kaiden. He was moving his hips and grinding on me and I felt myself getting wet. I was starting to regret not wearing panties. Every time he pressed himself against me, the material of the dress pressed against my pussy. I was getting horny and it made me remember that it had been months since I'd had sex. Kaiden was turning me on in a major way.

I turned around to face him so we were face to face. We kept on dancing but he stopped and pulled out his phone. He looked at whatever was on the screen, screwed his face up and then a look of panic took over his face.

"Everything alright?" I asked him.

He didn't respond to my question. In fact, he didn't say anything at all. He turned and walked away from me and I watched him walk out of the door. I was embarrassed as hell and I knew it was written all on my face. I was walking back over to the bar where Karla was when I spotted Jackson looking at me. He had a smug look on his face.

I rolled my eyes. Instead of heading back over to Karla to play third wheel, I decided to just take my ass home. Alone.

CHAPTER 4

Kaiden

I RUSHED OUT of the club, stepping into the warm Atlanta night. We'd been in the club for what seemed like forever but there was still a long ass line of people waiting outside who would never get in. They didn't understand how stuff like this worked. A party like that was just for the movers and the shakers, not the people who just wanted to get in.

I pulled my phone out of my pocket and sent a text to Brandon letting him know that I was leaving and taking a cab. I wished I was heading back to my house but I had somewhere to be.

I got a taxi from the long line of cars outside. As I got into one and began to pull off, I saw the girl I'd been dancing with, Remi, stepping out of the club. Damn, she was pretty.

As we drove, my mind snapped away from her though. I suddenly felt really self-conscious. I wondered how many people in the club had seen us dancing. Honestly, we got pretty hot and heavy but it wasn't anything that mostly everyone else in the club wasn't doing. I did have a real sense of guilt about it though. I wasn't trying to be that flirtatious with that girl but it just happened. Something about the atmosphere and the liquor had me going.

Because my family was African American and had money, we were kind of given a little privilege and shit. I wasn't a celebrity myself, but being one of the Briggs kids did get in me into certain places and people recognized me because I was friends with a lot of people in the world of entertainment. Word about my new relationship was spreading and I wasn't trying to have some shit get back to my woman.

I looked at my phone again as it went off. I'd gotten another text message, now adding to the list of the other ones on my screen. I shook my head and pushed thoughts of shorty from the club out of my head. I had other shit to attend to that night. It was nothing more or less than a dance in the club. I was drinking and that was it. I don't know why I was bugging out over it in the back of the cab.

I'd been dating my lady for about 6 months. I'd met Chloe Mack about a year ago. I'd recently invested in a new African American skin care line. I was looking for someone to help promote it in the right way. I asked around and people told me that Chloe Mack and her company had the best public relations and advertising in the South, especially if you were black.

I didn't specifically ask for a meeting with her though. I'd just wanted someone from the company to contact me. I was surprised when Chloe herself took the meeting. She told me that she'd heard that I was looking to get into business and she'd heard of me because of my last name and what my father did.

When I first met Chloe, I had to admit that I thought she was attractive but that was about it.

I was there for business and didn't want to mix the two of them at all. She was nice and very professional. I didn't know how old she was but I'd never been one of those people who liked older women like that.

Chloe had decided to take me as a client and she helped me to launch the skin care line and get it into a bunch of stores and even get some celebrity clientele. I was hype.

One night I'd gone to her office to drop off a bottle of champagne I bought her as a celebratory gift. I presented it to her and she told me she was thankful but she wasn't trying to drink it all alone.

Long story short, we ended up going through the entire bottle in her office and we fucked right there on her desk. It was...different. Chloe was about 15 years older than me and fucking her was different from other people. Not to sound like a creep but she was more seasoned than other women I'd been with, and I'd been with a lot of women.

She and I took it slow. I genuinely enjoyed Chloe's company. Being around her outside of a work setting was cool because it seemed like she'd been waiting to get around people that would let her let her guard down. She told me that she didn't really have much family besides an adopted niece, but that was it.

For the last six months, she and I had been dating and it'd been cool. But I think that's what it was that had gotten on my nerves. It was just alright. At times, I felt like I should have been dating someone closer to my age. I was definitely growing to love her and care about her more, but the spark that was initially there was fading and I didn't know what to do.

I wasn't the typical type of guy that Chloe dated. She told me that she'd been married twice and since neither marriage worked out, she'd just been playing the scene. I could tell that she was used to dating broke niggas that probably just fucked her right. When we first started dating, she kept trying to flex on me and pay for everything and also thought she had some kind of power over me if she did that. I had to check her a couple of times and let her know that my pockets weren't hurt at all. In fact, my family had more money than hers. But even in that, I think that was why I respected her so much. She told me how she'd taken her sister's company and built it up into what it was. I loved a hustler.

The cab slowed down as it pulled into Chloe's massive driveway. She lived in a large two story house with beautiful back and front yards. She had four bedrooms and 3 bathrooms. She didn't need that much space since it was just her and her dogs but she kept it.

I got out of the cab and headed inside, using my key to enter. I stepped into the large entrance hall of the house. Every time I went there I had to admit that it was a beautiful place.

Chloe was sitting in the kitchen. I walked in and saw her sitting at the large marble island style counter top.

"I was so worried about you when you didn't answer my calls," she said to me. She put down her glass of wine, hopped off her stool and walked over to me. She kissed me on the lips and I noticed she had on a face full of makeup. I didn't know who sat around with a full face at 3 in the morning but there she was. I never had the heart to tell her that I'd always preferred girls with less makeup. That was Chloe though. I think she felt like she needed to compete with the younger women who found me attractive.

I had to resist the urge to roll my eyes. Chloe had developed a nasty tendency to act like my mother instead of my girlfriend and I wasn't with the shits at all. She needed to chill.

"I'm fine," I said to her. I was still just standing there while she walked back over to keep drinking her glass of wine. "Why you up so late? And why you fully dressed?" Chloe was wearing a black dress that I'd seen her wear before. I had to admit that it looked good on her though.

"I was up waiting for you," she said. She turned to look at me. "You said you were coming over and I wanted to wait for you." She looked at me and I could tell she was horny. She always did stuff like that when she wanted some dick. "You wanna go upstairs?" She was looking me up and down like I was a buffet.

"Yeah, let's go," I said to her. She got up and walked over to me seductively. She grabbed me by the hand and let the way to her large bedroom.

Chloe wasted no time in pushing me on the bed and straddling me. She started kissing me on the lips and neck. I was kissing her back but my mind was elsewhere. I gripped Chloe's ass and my body was going through all the motions as if I was really interested in what we were about to do.

Sadly though, my mind slipped back to the shorty from the club. That chick Remi was beautiful and had a banging ass body. She could dance and I almost felt like I was gonna get hard after a couple of minutes of dancing with her, but I just chilled and kept dancing.

I could only admit it to myself and I hated to admit it but I was definitely gonna take her home at the end of the night if she was down. And with the way she was moving, she was down. I felt fucked up knowing I would have cheated, but I was also relieved it didn't get that far. I was a playboy for sure but I never wanted to cheat on someone I was cool with. I think that was all a part of the fading feelings or whatever it was for Chloe that I had.

As had become typical with our sex life, Chloe hadn't even noticed that I wasn't into it. I'd dropped my arms and was pretty much letting her do all the work.

Chloe had worked her way down my body

and she got to my belt buckle. She undid it and pulled at my underwear until my semi hard dick flopped out. Even though I wasn't all the way hard, it was still big.

She put her lips on it and began to go up and down on it. As she bobbed up and down on my dick, I closed my eyes. As fucked up as it was, I could see Remi moving up and down on my dick in my head. I pictured her soft, full lips moving around on my dick with all the spit that Chloe was using currently.

I felt like a fucking creep for real. I'd only known shorty from the club for a few minutes and here I was replacing Chloe with her in my head. I was pissed off with myself.

I pulled my dick out of Chloe's mouth and stood up. I stood up from bed and undressed, letting my clothes drop to the floor. I was there, naked. Once Chloe saw my clothes off, she did the same.

I turned her over on the bed roughly. She was on her stomach. I looked down at her ass and I pictured Remi's ass. I pulled out a condom from the nightstand and slipped it on. Chloe was already a little wet but I put some lube on the condom and slid myself into her.

The guilt that I was feeling about picturing Remi instead of Chloe was definitely fucking with me, which was why I just wanted to fuck her from behind.

"Ugh, Kaiden!" Chloe yelled my name out loud as I pumped myself in and out of her. I grabbed Chloe roughly by the hip and pumped my dick in and out of her. The sounds of our bodies slapping together were the only things to be heard in the room. I felt fucked up cause as much as I liked being around Chloe, I wondered what it'd be like to fuck Remi like that. Would her pussy be tighter? Would she moan the same way? I knew she was just a chick from the club but it had been so long since I'd been out and Remi had been the first person I'd danced with like that besides Chloe in forever.

We kept on going just like that for a while longer. The liquor in my system kept my dick hard. When I was done, I pulled out of Chloe and stepped back, breathing hard as hell. She slowly climbed up on the bed, clearly having enjoyed herself.

After I got rid of the condom, I climbed on the bed and she scooted over to me to lay on my chest.

"Damn baby," she said after kissing me on the cheek, "that was the best sex I've had in years." She got quiet like she was waiting for a response but I just pretended that I'd fallen asleep in the darkness. I was tired, but more than anything, I felt guilty for my thoughts.

CHAPTER 5

Remi

I'D GOTTEN to the office early the following day. I was making preparations for things to come and it was easier for me to work from the office instead of being at home. I was sitting behind my desk, answering emails, when Karla walked in. She was dressed a lot better than the night before, thankfully.

After that I went ahead and started sorting through some new designs. I had recently decided that I wanted to branch more into men's fashion so I was working on some stuff for that. I had some casual stuff as well as some suits all drawn up. I was now trying to match them up with possible fabrics. Stuff like that wasn't exciting to most people but I loved it. I was passionate about what I did.

"You're here early," she said, taking a seat in front of my desk. She handed me a cup of coffee and a few folders. "I went ahead and organized your meetings for the day."

"Good morning to you too, and thanks," I said to her. I'd been apprehensive about hiring my best friend as my assistant but Karla knew when to be professional and when to let her hair down and just be my friend.

"What's wrong with you?" Karla asked. She looked confused. "And what happened to you last night?" She leaned in close to me and smiled. "Did you go home with that fine ass Kaiden?"

I'd been in such a rush to leave that I didn't even tell Karla when I'd gone. "The ghost? No." I sat back in my chair and sighed. "So he and I were having a good time dancing and what not. I'm thinking everything is cool or whatever. Next thing I know, he pulls out his phone and the nigga is gone. I was standing there looking stupid."

Karla shook her head and then burst out

laughing. She was clearly amused. "Girl look, I know it's been a while since you been out on the town but that happens sometimes. Guys do it to girls, girls do it guys. It just happens."

The look on my face showed that I clearly wasn't feeling her response. "I mean...I know stuff like that happens from time to time, but still." I shook my head. She wasn't getting it.

"Well, it at least worked out for one of us," Karla said. "I got his brother Brandon's number. He was cute too. A year younger than me but nothing too bad. He seems like a nice guy."

"That's good for you," I said. I smiled at her. I knew she was trying to change the subject but I was over it. I knew it was childish, but still. I was really annoyed with that shit from the night before.

Karla sat back in the chair and sighed. "Ok girl, tell me the whole story."

"Like I said, he and I were just dancing and stuff. We were having a great time. We danced for what seemed like forever," I said.

"Girl I know," Karla said. "Brandon and I were watching y'all and waiting for you to finish and when y'all didn't, we just kept on talking."

"So like I said, he vanished after getting a

message or something on his phone. I don't really know. I was mad because I was standing there and stuff and Jackson spotted me. His ass looked so happy that I was alone again. I was over it," I exhaled deeply. "I know I don't have a right to be annoyed or anything but he and I really hit it off. We talked for a while and then started dancing. I was really enjoying myself and it seemed like he was too. After that I wasn't about to go and play third wheel with you and Brandon so I went and got a cab and took my ass home."

"There could have been any number of reasons why his ass left," Karla said sympathetically. "Shit, if his ass getting messages or phone calls that late, he probably had a girl to go home to. He left his brother and all that so who knows."

I nodded. She was making sense. It could have been any reason why he left. I didn't want to sit there and stress over it. Sometimes shit like that just happened. You meet someone and think y'all clicked and you just didn't.

"Besides," Karla went on, "you got a chance to make Jackson jealous and that counts for something."

"Oh please," I said. "His ass was putting on a show himself. He was throwing money at bottle girls and shit. He had a whole flock of bitches around him. Nothing but birds."

"But his ass was still focused on you though," Karla said with a smirk. I also smiled at that. It was true. He could make it seem like he was as unbothered as he wanted but he still cared.

Jackson and I had broken up a few months ago. On the surface, Jackson seemed to be the perfect catch. He was handsome, intelligent, kind, and could carry on a conversation. But beneath that, he had his own issues. Jackson and I dated for a little over a year, and it was great in the beginning, but after a while I started to notice how controlling and jealous he could be. He knew that because of what I did for a living and who my aunt was that I would always have to be in the industry, but he tried to control me. Everything I wore was too short or too sexy for him. He hated it when I talked to guys, despite the majority of them being my clients. I didn't understand how he could be so insecure since I'd never given him a reason to be.

"You're right about that," I said to her.

"I know," she said. "But girl, life goes on. That was one club. One time. We can always go out and find other people to get you out of this rut your ass is in. Shit, we could do something tonight if you wanted. I know of another spot we could go to."

"Tonight is no good," I said.

"Why not?"

"I have my Aunt Chloe's charity gala tonight," I said. A few years after my parents died and Aunt Chloe took over the company, she'd started a charity organization. The organization raised money for underprivileged kids in Georgia and sent them to camp each summer where they learned to use the arts. I supported it, but over the years I'd attended so many galas, parties, fundraisers and more that they all seemed to just turn into one long event in my head.

"Oh God," Karla said. "Is it time for that again? Just skip it. You know they used to be fun when we were young but now they're boring. I mean...dressing up is nice and stuff, don't get me wrong, but those things be so dry."

"Girl, I know," I said to her. "But you know I can't miss it for the world. I try to support

Aunt Chloe in everything she does. You know how much she did for me."

"Yeah, that's true," Karla said. "Have fun."

"I'll try," I said.

The rest of the day went by quickly. I'd managed to get a lot of work done, so much that I ended up going home a little earlier than usual. It worked out anyway since I'd need time to get myself ready for the gala. Aunt Chloe had a strict black tie dress code for the event so I had to make sure that I was dressed in my best.

It was like she knew that I was thinking of her. I got out the shower and Aunt Chloe called my cell phone.

"Hello," I answered after a few rings.

"Hello Remi, how are you?" Aunt Chloe sounded excited. "What are you up to?"

"Just got out the shower," I said. "I'm about to put on my makeup and get dressed. What about you?"

"I'm going over last minute details for the event," she said. "I'm so excited! We have so many donors coming and I'm sure everyone is going to have their checkbooks open to donate."

"Of course," I said. "The always do."

"True," Aunt Chloe said. "Now, I have some news. I'd like you to meet my new boyfriend."

I tried to sound excited when I spoke again. "Really? That's so exciting." I guess I did a good job at pretending to be excited for her. Either that or she was on such a high that she didn't notice my lack of enthusiasm.

Aunt Chloe had two failed marriages under her belt and told me she didn't plan on getting married again. She was at a point now where she had 'boyfriends' as she called them. They were nothing more than boy toys though. They came around, stuck with her for a little bit while she tricked on them and then they moved on. She had money and could usually find some little hood rat to pick up and clean off. It sounded rough but that's how it was. She'd been telling me about his latest one for longer than the others but all it meant was that she was taking more time with him than with the others. I was sure that in a few days or weeks, he'd be gone like the rest of them and she'd be on to the next.

"I know. I hope you guys hit it off. He's younger than me, but you know your aunt can keep up with the best of them," she said, throwing in a laugh, clearly amused at herself. "Well I've got to run, dear. I'll see you tonight."

"Ok," I said before clicking off the phone.

I sat in front of the vanity mirror in my room and put on my makeup. I wasn't the biggest fan of makeup so I kept it as light as possible, only putting on a little bit and sticking to a more natural look. I'd found the perfect shade of red lipstick to put on and I applied it. My hair was long as hell and I hadn't planned on doing anything with it. I pulled it back into a tight ponytail and tied it. I checked out my face and hair in the mirror. It was all coming together nicely.

I got dressed. I'd been working on a red-carpet dress for a client who had to cancel on me. I kept working on the dress and finished it, happy that it looked as good on me as I'd envisioned it looking on her. The dress was burgundy and long. In the front, there was a long slit that extended from my thigh on down. I'd gotten the idea for that part from seeing Angelina Jolie a few years ago. Plus, since I was short, it'd help me look taller. The waist of the dress was cinched with jewel embellishments and the top had the same design. The back of the dress was open from my neck to just above my butt. After I was all the way dressed, with black heels of course, I checked myself out. I looked good. I hated that the event would most likely be boring but I was fine with going to support my aunt.

I headed outside, where I had a car waiting for me. I got in the back and we headed to the space where the event would be. It was at some large event hall in one of the more affluent neighborhoods. If there was anything that Aunt Chloe could do, it was put on an event.

I know it sounded strange but even as we drove to the event, I couldn't help but put the events of the night before out of my head. I knew it was weird for me to be so hung up on Kaiden but I was. I know it was only a little conversation and a dance but it seemed like there was potential there that I wanted to explore. It was like he was Cinderella or something the way he rushed off. Whatever though. I pushed it out of my mind.

The driver pulled up outside of the event and opened the door for me. I stepped out and saw that my aunt had hired some people to take photos. I got inside the place and into the welcoming hall where I posed for some pictures before heading all the way inside. I thought about getting a drink from the open bar but decided against it.

I said hello to a couple of people that I knew. I thanked them for coming out. Even though it wasn't my event, people knew whose niece I was so I made sure to play my part.

I spotted my aunt after a while. Her back was towards me but I did see that she had someone on her arm. It must have been her latest boyfriend. I couldn't believe she'd brought him to an event. It wasn't something she'd done before. I walked up to her and tapped her on the shoulder.

"Hi Aunty," I said. She turned around to face me and I was shocked when the person on her arms turned around.

"I'd like you to meet my boyfriend, Kaiden," Aunt Chloe said in a proud way. I was shocked and tried not to let it show on my face. Standing there, dressed exquisitely in a black suit and tie, was none other than Kaiden. I couldn't figure out what to say. I hoped Aunt Chloe hadn't noticed.

CHAPTER 6

Kaiden

OF ALL THE people in the whole wide world for me to meet and bump and grind with at the club, I had to end up dancing with Chloe's niece? I swear that certain things only happened to me. I might have been making a big deal out of it though. It was really nothing more than a dance. Still, the chances of that happening were both shocking and amazing and I couldn't believe it. Those were the thoughts that went through my head as I stood there in front of Remi.

The shock of the situation also registered on Remi's face. Chloe didn't seem to notice anything wrong but I knew that if one of us didn't say something, she might get suspicious. I extended my hand to her, hoping that she'd play along.

"Nice to meet you," I said to Remi. I extended my hand and she took it and began to shake it.

"Hi, I'm Remi, nice to meet you too," Remi said. My heart slowed down just a little bit, glad that she was playing along with me.

Chloe smiled and planted a kiss on my cheek. "It's so nice to have the two most important people in my life finally come together in one room. So Kaiden, Remi is 23 years old. She grew up working at the company originally started by my sister before she died, but now she's doing her own thing."

"And what's that?" I asked because I was trying to keep playing along with what was happening, but I did have a real interest in learning more about Remi. I didn't know what it was that I found so attractive or mysterious about her, but I wanted to learn more.

"She's an artist...kind of," Chloe said. "Since a young age, she's been interested in fashion and all of that, so I encouraged her a couple of years ago to start up a line. So she's done just that and more." Chloe smiled, clearly impressed with Remi. She turned to her. "She's not little Remi anymore. She's Remi Montell, fashion designer and wardrobe stylist. And if her line keeps being as popular as it is, she'll be even better off. She's self-made. Yeah, she got a start because of the company and the name that her parents started but she made a way for herself. I'm proud of her for that."

"Thanks Aunt Chloe," said Remi with sincerity in her voice. "I really appreciate it."

"It's the truth," said Chloe. She sighed and looked around the room. "Well, I have to make my rounds. I need to go and make sure that everyone is fine and that people are making donations. Later on, I'll give my usual address. I hope that the two of you can keep yourselves entertained." She smiled again and kissed me. This time it was a peck on the lips. She walked away, leaving Remi and I standing there not saying anything while music played in the background.

"Do you want to grab a seat?" I asked her. I looked around at the tables that were all around. We had seats designated for us but it was still cocktail hour so we could sit wherever we wanted for a while longer.

"Sure," she said. We walked over to a table and sat down. An awkward silence fell between us.

"So," Remi began, "I had no idea that you and my aunt were...dating." Remi was looking at me awkwardly. I knew she didn't know what to say. Hell, neither did I. It wasn't like we'd fucked or anything like that, but I was definitely feeling her. I didn't know what it was about the situation that was making it awkward, but it was.

"Yeah," I said awkwardly. "Yeah we are. I didn't know you were her niece either."

"I figured that out," Remi said. "I knew she'd been dating someone for a few months but I clearly didn't know it was you. I wouldn't have danced with you if I'd have known. I try not to get involved in my aunt's personal stuff like that. She can be a lot to handle at times."

"Yeah, I figured," I said. It got quiet between us again. "So what's up with you?" I looked at her in her eyes, trying to figure her out.

"What you mean?" She asked me.

"I mean just in general," I said. "I don't know too many people here, at least I don't know nobody here well enough to try and talk to 'em, so I guess I'm stuck with you." I said it in a serious voice but then smirked. She laughed. Damn, she had a nice smile.

"What you wanna know about me?" She was staring at me like I was the only person in the room. It was weird to me because Chloe never really looked at me like that. It kind of always felt like I was something on her to do list as opposed to her boyfriend.

"Anything you want to tell me," I said.

"Well, my aunt touched on all of the major things. I'm into fashion and styling people. I got into it because it's something I'm really passionate about. What about you?"

"Well, I'm a part of the Briggs family," I said. I waited for some kind of response but she didn't say anything, which kind of surprised me. Most people automatically knew who my family was once I said my last name.

"Is that supposed to mean something?" She was looking at me like she was waiting for me to say something else.

I smiled. I wasn't about to try and do the

whole 'don't you know who I am?' thing. It was actually a nice surprise to know that she wasn't familiar with us. "You know the computer and software company? Briggs? That's us," I said to her.

Recognition crossed Remi's face and she nodded. "Oh, ok," she said while nodding. "I've definitely heard of that company. You guys are big time, huh?"

"Something like that," I said. "It's my father's company, really. But as the oldest, I'm next in line to run the company. I also got my own stuff I'm working on."

"Why?" Remi was looking confused.

"Why what?" I asked.

"Why are you working on your own stuff?" She paused. "I mean...if I was the son of the head of a major corporation, I would probably just sit back and relax and stuff."

"That's not true," I said to her.

"What makes you say that?"

"Cause you and I are in similar positions," I told her. "I got my father and you got your aunt. But even though we could both sit back and not do anything, we both still have other things that we're working on. We hustlers."

"That's true," Remi said. "I hadn't even thought of it like that." She was nodding her head in approval. I wondered what was going through her head.

Remi and I stood there for what seemed like forever just talking and getting to know one another better. The more I got to know her, the more she impressed me. She was young but ambitious and wasn't out there trying to get any handouts.

Something else was happening too and I needed to think about what I was doing. We'd somehow began to flirt with one another and I didn't mind it one bit. I knew it was wrong but I was getting so caught up in the moment that I couldn't help it.

"Do you want a drink?" I asked Remi. I wanted to get a couple of minutes away from her to get my thoughts together. The night could really go one of two ways and I wanted to make sure that I was thinking about it with clear mind before it went the way that I wanted it to.

"Sure," Remi said. "What are you drinking?"

"Probably whiskey," I said to her.

She nodded with approval. "Not my go to, but I'll have whatever you're having."

I turned and walked away, headed towards the bar. I spotted Chloe on the other side of the room, chatting away with some woman. She was in her own world. The bartender placed the two drinks in front of me and I put some cash in his tip jar. I walked back over to where Remi was waiting and handed her the glass.

"Thanks," she said. She took a sip of the generously poured whiskey and closed her eyes. It was clear she was trying her best not to make a face or something. I started laughing.

"What's so funny?" she asked me.

"You," I said as I took a sip of my own drink. "You over there trying to pretend it's not affecting you the way it is. It's clearly stronger than what you're used to. I can get you something else if you want."

She narrowed her eyes at me and shook her head. "I'm fine," she said. She threw back the rest of the drink in one big gulp.

"Damn girl, slow down," I said to her. I took the glass from her and finished my own drink before giving the glasses to a waiter who was walking by.

"I'm fine," she repeated. The liquor must have been working on her because even though she didn't seem to be tense before, she definitely loosened up some more.

"I see," I said to her. I looked her up and down. When my eyes met with hers it was clear that she'd noticed me looking at her but didn't seem to have a problem with it.

"So, I was thinking that I should have your number," I said to her. I didn't know what had gotten into me but I wasn't about to try and stop it. The liquor was working on the two of us and we both knew it. There was also a very real attraction between us that seemed to be growing.

"Oh really?" She asked. "Why should you have it?"

"You know I have events and things to go to," I said to her. "It'd be nice to have someone to style me for some events and stuff. You know." I smiled at her and she smiled back.

"Ok, that sounds cool," she said. I handed her my phone and watched her punch in the numbers before handing it back to me. I put it in my pocket and looked around. I wanted to make sure that no one saw anything between us.

I was feeling mischievous but didn't need any extra eyes on me.

"So," Remi began, "I liked dancing with you the other night." She placed her elbows on the table and put her face in her hands. She looked at me with her eyes a little lower than they were before. Yeah, the alcohol was taking effect.

"Me too," I said to her as I leaned in closer to her.

"I liked the way you touched me," she said to me. "I hadn't been out in a long time so it was nice to dance with somebody the way we danced."

"Oh really?" I smiled at her again. I glanced around and over my shoulders to make sure no one was looking. I reached under the table and brushed my hand over Remi's leg. Her skin was smooth. She closed her eyes as my hand went over the smoothness of her skin.

"Damn," she said out loud. She raised a hand like she was going to try and stop me but didn't.

I'd been around a lot of women in my life so I knew whenever they were turned on. Remi was definitely turned on by me. She was staring at me like I was a piece of prime rib and she couldn't wait to take a bite. I knew what we were doing was dangerous but I also knew that I wasn't in the mood to stop.

"Did you want to go somewhere else so we could talk?" I asked her. I removed my hand from her leg and looked at her.

"Yes," Remi said with a grin.

CHAPTER 7

Remi

When the night first started, I prepared myself for yet another boring gala thrown by my aunt. Coming into it, I just knew that it was going to be dry as hell and I'd end up being bored to death. However, it had all taken a turn for the better after the shock I received. I didn't know that Kaiden was my Aunt Chloe's new boyfriend. I would have never guessed it in a million years.

When I realized exactly who he was and what was going on, I was shocked but couldn't really show it on my face. I wasn't trying to raise any suspicions with Aunt Chloe. Beyond that though, Kaiden and I had only danced. It wasn't like he and I had much time to really build anything between us. We'd done some flirting but I was trying to push it from my mind.

After Aunt Cloe left me with Kaiden, I didn't know what to expect from him. It was a different setting. We weren't in the club and weren't drunk so it had me wondering if whatever connection there might have been between us was still there. I was pleasantly surprised by Kaiden.

He spoke a lot about himself and the things he wanted in life. He reminded me a lot of myself and I think that was what had drawn me to him. He spoke with a certain passion that I didn't see in too many people. Beyond all of that though, Kaiden was handsome as fuck. I hated that he was with my Aunt Chloe because the more he and I sat and talked, the more I realized I was attracted to him.

Kaiden was sweet without coming across as soft. I loved that he was a hardworking person. I came from a family of people who worked really hard for the things they wanted and I'd always known that I couldn't be with someone who didn't work just as hard as me. I liked that even though he could have just been a spoiled rich kid and spend his father's money, Kaiden had the drive to want better for himself.

I knew that there was a line and Kaiden and I were dangerously close to crossing it. I didn't want to but the more that he and I sat next to one another and talked, the more I realized that he and I were much better off than him and my aunt. But I wasn't about to try and cross that line with him. I was never the type to take a man from a woman, but after the way that he touched me, I knew that I wanted to borrow him...just for the night of course. What my aunt didn't know wouldn't hurt her. Plus, having a little fun with Kaiden would probably be the best way for me to move on with my life. I knew it was wrong but Kaiden and I were getting so caught up in the moment.

Kaiden and I looked around, noticing that pretty much everyone at the event was involved in their own conversations and not paying us any mind. I spotted Aunt Chloe talking to a man and woman on the other side of the table. The gala had been going on for a while so I knew it was almost time for her to give her annual address. Each year she gave a speech thanking people for coming and donating and blah, blah, blah. I hadn't heard every variation of it over the years and even though she switched it up, it always sounded the same to me.

The event hall had a large entrance hallway and another hall way off to the side. We walked slowly, trying not to draw any attention to us. I was kind of tipsy and it seemed like he was as well. We weren't touching one another but we were giggling like school kids as we made our way out one of the side doors towards the side hallway. My heart was beating fast with the thought of getting caught. I knew that what we were doing was fucked up, but more than anything it felt fun. I knew we were being reckless but I was always the person who kept it together all the time, so it felt good to release and just live life on the wild side for once.

We disappeared out into the hall where there were large windows with huge draping curtains that were red. They went from the ceiling to the floor. I turned around and noticed that the door we had just left had a very clear view of about half the tables in the room where the gala was.

"We should go somewhere else," I said. I wasn't trying to get caught. Kaiden just held his hands up to his mouth to get me to shush. He pulled back the curtain and stepped behind it. He held his hand up and waved to me, inviting me to come behind it with him. I followed him.

It felt like I'd been waiting for all of forever to do it but Kaiden and I finally started to kiss. His full lips came down to mine and the two of us kissed for what seemed like forever. His large hand started feeling up my leg. I was glad that I'd worn the dress with the big slit in the leg. It was easy access for him.

Kaiden knew that he was teasing me and I was so turned on by it. His hand slowly traveled up my leg towards my sweet spot. His large fingers got close to my pussy and he pressed against it from the outside through my panties. I was already wet but him playing with me had made me even wetter. I had to close my mouth to stop myself from moaning. I didn't realize until then how horny I was and how I'd missed having male attention.

Kaiden kept playing with me. He slipped my

panties to the side and when I thought I wouldn't be able to take it anymore, he took his fingers and started to put them inside of me one at a time. He put in one finger and began to slowly massage inside of me. He pulled it out and brought it up to his face where he licked his finger, letting my sweet, sticky juices hang on his tongue before he closed his mouth. He then went back inside of me with the same finger. He moved on to using two fingers and then before I knew it, he'd inserted three fingers inside of me and was moving them around inside of me like an expert. His fingers were moving inside of me like I was a piano and he was trying to play a song.

I opened my mouth and let out a soft moan. Kaiden raised his other hand and covered my mouth and grinned. He knew what he was doing for sure.

It must have been time for Aunt Chloe to give her address. I heard her on the microphone asking for people to get to their seats. There was a shuffling of chairs and then silence. I knew Aunt Chloe had to be standing in front of the crowd of people, waiting to begin her speech.

"Good evening ladies and gentlemen," Aunt

Chloe's voice came through the speaker, "I am so thankful and pleased that you all have decided to join me again for yet another gala benefiting my charity organization." She paused while people applauded. If I knew my aunt, she was loving all the attention she was getting from the people who'd gathered.

Kaiden's fingers were still moving around inside of me. His free hand was still over my mouth and I was trying my hardest not to moan. If I got too loud, I was sure that someone inside the hall would hear us. The danger of the situation was turning me on even more. I was already wet but Kaiden and the fact that we could get caught at any time was making me wetter. I felt my juices begin to trickle slowly down my leg.

"When I first began my organization, I wanted to help out people who'd grown up the same way that I did; poor, non-privileged, and in need of help," Aunt Chloe's voice came back over the speaker system. "My sister, God rest her soul, and I had always known that we wanted to help out others and give back to a community that helped us out. If it wasn't for people doing things like I'm doing now, we would have been a lot less well off."

I could hear Aunt Chloe continuing to talk but her words were nothing more than background noise for what was going on behind the curtain with Kaiden. I'd forgotten all about feeling any guilt about what I was doing. I was much too caught up in the fact that I was feeling amazing and wanted nothing more than to keep going. If Kaiden's hands were as amazing as this, I wondered what the man could do with other parts of his body.

Kaiden started licking on my neck and I had to cover my own damn mouth to stop myself from moaning louder. It felt that good. He moved his tongue up until he was by my ear and started to lick and bite on it. He was whispering all types of shit in my ear about what he wanted to do to me and in that moment, I'd let him do whatever he wanted.

"Damn Remi, you so wet," he whispered in my ear. He was more than right. I couldn't recall the last time I'd been this wet. Even being with Jackson I didn't get this turned on. His sex was good but he never prolonged the foreplay the way that Kaiden was doing to me then. The mix of the danger of the situation and the fact that I was so attracted to Kaiden were doing things to me.

"I sincerely appreciate all of you for coming tonight. Whether you are returning guests or people that I met for the first time tonight, your time, and donations are more than appreciated. I want you all to know that I value each of you but more importantly, every dollar that you donate puts a smile on the face of a child who may have had to go without," Aunt Chloe said.

There was something turning me on about the fact that she was and everyone else were just feet inside the room and I was hiding behind a curtain, doing something I shouldn't have been doing.

I decided that I wanted to take control of the situation. I took a step back and pulled Kaiden's hand out of me. It felt good but I wanted something to move on to the next thing.

I started pulling at the front of Kaiden's pants. I felt like I was hungry and his dick was the only thing that could feed me. I undid his belt and zipped own his zipper. There wasn't much light behind the curtain but the moon outside was shining through the window, illuminating us. The bulge in his black boxer briefs was big as hell. I ran my hand across his six pack abs and followed his happy trail down to his dick. I pulled out his big dick and watched as it flopped, still semi-hard out of his underwear.

"Damn," I said.

"You like what you see?" He was looking at me like he was proud of himself. Shit, I would be too if I was a guy who had a dick as big as that one. It had to be at least 7 inches already and was still growing.

I didn't respond to him. I hiked my dress up so I could get down and I dropped to my knees. I could only imagine the image if someone caught us. He had on a black suit and tie and I was wearing and evening gown but there I was, taking his dick into my throat like a fucking champ.

I started off slow, grabbing his dick and putting it into my mouth. I was glad that he had no smell down there. Too many guys didn't know enough about cleanliness and had weird odors and stuff. My mouth was wet as hell as I took all of Kaiden into my mouth. If this experience with him was only going to happen one night only then I needed to make sure that it was something that Kaiden remembered.

Now we'd switched places. He was the one trying not to moan. I was putting it on him. I felt drool dripping down both sides of my mouth as I bobbed my neck up and down on his dick. I massaged his balls with my free hand, trying to make sure he felt as good as he'd made me fee. He threw his head back and took a step back to lean against the window. It was clear he was enjoying it as much as I was.

Kaiden grabbed the back of my head gently and began to thrust himself in and out of my mouth. I was glad he wasn't messing up my hair. It seemed trivial but I needed to still get out of there and look normal. I felt like some type of porn bitch or something because for every thrust he gave, I made sure to meet it. I wasn't about to slip up and let his ass take control again, at least not until I was ready to. I could hear Aunt Chloe's speech in the background. I was glad that she was so long winded because it gave us a good amount of time to do what we were doing.

"Nah, I can't wait any longer," said Kaiden. I didn't know what he meant but I got the meaning a few seconds later. Kaiden grabbed me and stood me up. He started kissing me again and pulled up my dress, making sure not to rip or tear it. I was thankful that I'd made the dress with a little spandex so it could fit over my curves. If not, Kaiden might have torn the whole thing.

He lifted my dress up until it was around my waist and pulled my panties off of me. His dick was hard as a rock. He reached into his back pocket and pulled out a condom. I watched him slide it onto his big ass dick and I was afraid that the condom might break as it stretched over it.

Once the condom was all the way on, Kaiden took me and position me so that I was sitting on the windowsill. He moved himself closer and closer and closer to me until he was right in front of me. His dick slowly slid into me. He stretched out my pussy since it was so wide. I gripped on to the back of Kaiden's head as he pumped himself in and out of me. I was trying not to make any noise but it was difficult because it felt so damn good.

"Oh my god," Kaiden moaned into my ear. "This shit so tight."

"Fuck me," I moaned into Kaiden's ear.

It sounded like my aunt was close to ending her speech and I knew we needed to be done with our little romp before anybody started to notice we were gone. Kaiden started to pump himself in and out of my quicker. Our bodies were making noises but we couldn't hide the sounds of our skin slapping together.

"So, ladies and gentlemen," my Aunt Chloe's voice said loudly, "with all that being said, enjoy yourself. We have enough food and liquor to get your wallets open and to make sure that you all leave here full, drunk, and happy!" The crowd laughed and then began to clap and cheer loudly.

At the same time that they cheered, I was making noises of my own. As the crowd began to yell, I was cumming all over Kaiden's dick. I'd whispered that we needed to hurry up and he pushed himself in and out of my quickly. As the clapping began, I felt Kaiden explode into the condom and my own body began to shake with an orgasm.

Kaiden was breathing deeply into my ear as he backed off of me. I hopped down off the ledge and began to fix myself. He started to get his clothes together too. We'd have to sneak back into the party and make it look like we hadn't gone anywhere.

Kaiden finished getting himself together before I did. "See you out there," he said smoothly. He winked at me before peeking out from behind the curtain. I stayed behind there a few more minutes. In case anyone was watching, I didn't want it to be too obvious that he and I were coming out of the same place. Besides that, I needed time to fix my clothes. I wanted to make sure I didn't look like I'd just had sex.

After I got myself together, I peeked out from behind the curtain and saw that the coast was clear. I walked out from behind it and came back in from another door because I didn't want to be seen coming in from the side door as well. I effortlessly rejoined the crowd of people and started making small talk with a couple of people I knew.

I knew that I should be feeling guilty. I knew that I should have been beating myself up with guilt over what I'd done and I should have probably been feeling fear that Aunt Chloe would find out and what would happen then. I knew I should have been feeling a lot of things.

But I wasn't.

As I mixed and mingled with people, I searched my brain and my mind for a little bit of the guilt that I should have felt but it wasn't there. I couldn't figure out why though. I think it had to do with the fact that I knew my Aunt Chloe and how she ran through guys. She was never the type to hold on to men for a long time, despite the two short lived marriages she'd been through. Yeah, her fling with Kaiden had lasted longer than a lot of her other ones but it was still just that; a fling. I wasn't expecting it to last much longer than beyond tonight.

I also didn't feel any guilt because I liked Kaiden. The more that he and I talked, the more I realized how much better he'd be with me. I wasn't trying to take him from Aunt Chloe though. I just wanted to borrow him for the night and I'd succeeded in doing it. I knew it was wrong but I also knew that we could just leave it where it was.

I made my rounds, making sure to speak to as many people as possible. I wanted to be nice and visible so that in case anyone asked, they could just say that they'd seen me at the party. I didn't need any gaps in time where I was missing so that people could start to wonder where I'd been.

While walk across the room my phone went off. I pulled it out and saw it was a text message from a number that I didn't recognize. I opened it and saw that it was Kaiden.

Hey, it's Kaiden. I was thinking that we should go out tomorrow? What you think?

Was he asking me on a date? It seemed like that was what was happening. Damn, sleeping with Kaiden was one thing but going on a date with him was something else entirely. Like I said before, I wasn't trying to steal him or anything, but he was making it hard not to leave him alone.

I'm down. I sent the text in reply after thinking about it for a few seconds. I didn't know what had gotten into me, but fuck it. If he wanted to go on a date, I'd go. I knew my Aunt Chloe and knew that she was going to be moving on from Kaiden soon enough. The thing about her was that she always had someone else waiting. Before she moved on from one guy, she usually had the next one lined up. Kaiden would be no different.

Cool, came the text reply from Kaiden. *I don't*

know what it is about you but I'm feeling you. I know it sounds crazy but I feel a connection to you.

I couldn't help but smile. I was feeling the same thing. I read the message again before putting my phone back into my clutch. I didn't want to walk around texting all night. It might have been suspicious. I knew it was fucked up but the next day I'd be going on a date with my Aunt's man. I wanted to get to know Kaiden and figure out what he was all about. He seemed like a nice guy and I wanted to get to know him in a regular setting as opposed to something rushed like the last two times we'd met.

CHAPTER 8

Kaiden

I'D ENJOYED the party in more ways than one. My little romp with Remi had been some of the best sex I'd had in forever. Older women like Chloe had it going on but there was something about Remi and the way she moved. I loved her tight body. I wanted to see what it would be like to have a real rendezvous with her as opposed to the rush job that happened behind the curtain. It didn't matter though, 'cause that was enough for me.

I'd also managed to do some work-related stuff as well. Although Chloe was trying treat me like I was some boytoy of hers, I had to establish with people that I was my own man. Once I put out there that I was Kaiden Briggs, people started to listen. I'd known a few people that were there through my business dealings but I'd also met a lot of people and given out and collected a lot of business cards. As my father always said, "Networking happens everywhere and anywhere."

I was sitting in the back of the limousine with Chloe. She wasn't nearly as drunk as I had hoped she'd be so I knew she would be trying to get some from me later and I wasn't in the mood, especially not after I felt so drained because of Remi. I was staring out the window, trying not to look distracted while I listened to Chloe go on about the party.

"I had so much fun," she said. She sounded so pleased with herself. "I was so glad that everything came together the way that it did."

"Me too," I chimed in absentmindedly.

"Did you have a chance to meet Mr. Wolf?" she asked me.

"I'm not sure," I said. "What did he look like?"

She sucked her teeth. "He had a bald head and white eyebrows, very distinguished looking.

I liked his first wife more than his current one though. He was asking me about you. He said his company is looking for a new technology provider and I told him about you."

"Thank you," I said. I turned my head from the window and faced her. She was looking at me with confusion all over her face. "What?" I asked.

"You just seem distracted," she said to me as she eyed me suspiciously. "How did you and Remi hit it off?"

Stupidly, I didn't just answer the question. I opened my mouth to speak and then closed it. Then I started coughing. Finally, I opened my mouth and spoke. "She was cool."

I knew I'd fucked up then because Chloe was looking at me funny as hell. "What does that mean? Why are you acting so funny?"

I had to cover my tracks. I knew I'd fucked up already by acting so dumb when she asked me about Remi. "No reason," I said coolly. "Remi was cool. After you left, she and I had an interesting conversation about her fashion and stuff. She's a lot like you, very ambitious."

"Sounds good," Chloe said. She seemed to relax some. If there was anything Chloe liked, it was a compliment. Just like I'd hoped, she seemed to take the bait. "Remi is nice. She takes after me a lot."

I just nodded, not trying to open my mouth and make Chloe any more suspicious than she'd been before.

The car arrived at Chloe's house and we headed inside. I told her I was tired and I wanted to go take a shower. She headed up to the bedroom.

While in the shower, I was scrubbing the hell out of my skin. I wanted to make sure that I had no traces of Remi on me. I knew I didn't since Chloe had been sitting next to me in the car and didn't say anything, but the guilt of the situation was making me scrub harder. I got out of the shower and put on some basketball shorts that I kept at Chloe's house.

I walked into the bedroom and saw that Chloe hadn't fallen asleep as I hoped. Between the guilt I was feeling and the fact that Remi had pretty much drained all of the sexual energy from me, I hoped she didn't want to have sex. But when as I looked at her laying on the bed in a sexy nightgown and peeped the look in her eyes, I knew what she wanted. I tried not to make eye contact as I walked around her to head to the other side of the bed. I laid down on top of the covers and turned the light off on my side of the bed. She did the same.

Within seconds, I felt Chloe making moves to get closer to me. Her leg rolled up on mine and she started placing gentle kisses all on my neck and chest. She moved to try and put herself on top of me and I used my hand to stop her.

"What?" She was clearly annoyed and I could hear it in her voice.

"I'm tired," I said to her. "You know I was working all day and then I came to your event. I'm too tired, but I got you in the morning." I kissed her on the forehead and then yawned for dramatic effect.

"Are you serious?" Chloe asked. The anger was apparent in her voice.

"Baby, I'll take care of you in the morning for sure," I said.

Chloe didn't say anything. She just rolled all the way over to her side of the bed and pulled the covers up over her. A few minutes later I heard the sounds of her sleeping. She'd be alright. I, on the other hand, wasn't.

I would have liked to just roll over and head to sleep but I couldn't. Laying there in the dark, I had so many thoughts in my mind.

Part of me wanted to wake Chloe up and tell her all about what had happened. I knew that the right thing to do would be to just confess. But I knew I couldn't just do that, no matter how much I wanted to.

I was sure my relationship with Chloe would be over if I told her about what happened with Remi. I could deal with that, though. We'd only been dating for six months and I could walk away just as easily as I could stay.

I knew telling Chloe wasn't the thing to do because of Remi. Remi and Chloe were family. They loved one another. It'd probably destroy their relationship if Chloe found out about us. I wasn't about to ruin what they had going on.

I turned over to my side, hoping that my mind would quiet itself and let me go to sleep, but it wasn't happening. I lay there thinking about Remi and all the things I wanted to do to her and with her. It was fucked up, I know, but I couldn't get her off my mind. I wanted to see her again. I wanted to touch her again. I wanted to be inside her again.

Don't get me wrong, Chloe was good in the bedroom. She knew what she was doing and could ride the hell out of me. But the way that Remi turned me on and made me hard without even trying was something else. I was also amazed that she was down for our freaky little fun earlier behind the curtain. I liked the excitement she brought to me. Chloe was less spontaneous and didn't excite me in that way.

The longer I laid there, the more I realized I wanted to get to know Remi more. Her personality was great and it seemed like she had a lot going for herself. I was attracted to her physically but I realized that there was so much more to her than that. I wanted to get to know her more, which was why I'd asked her to go on the date. I knew we were playing it dangerous by going out, but I wanted to get to know her. I had to see her again.

I'd finally been able to drift off to sleep and managed to sleep a few hours of sleep in. When I got up the next morning, Chloe was already gone. I knew that she still had an attitude because she didn't say anything to me. I checked my phone and she hadn't sent a text or anything either. She'd be fine.

I went ahead and got dressed and headed to work. I kept some clothes at Chloe's house since I was there so often. I got to work and began my day. I had to admit that I was preoccupied with my own thoughts for most of the day. I was heading out with Remi later on that day and I wanted to make sure that everything went right.

A little after lunchtime, I was in one of the boardrooms in the office, giving a presentation on a new product that was going to boost sales. All day I'd been distracted with thoughts of what I was going to be doing later.

"So," I continued my presentation, "if you will all turn to page five, you'll see the figures I just spoke about." All six of the people at the table, including my father, turned the page.

I fucked up then because my mind slipped to Remi and I fucked up some of the figures I was supposed to be sharing.

"So, as you can see, I'm expecting this to boost sales by 20%," I said to them.

"Where is that listed?" asked one of the men. He was looking down at his packet and flipping the pages back and forth and then looking up at me.

"What do you mean?" I asked. I walked

over the desk and picked up my packet. I flipped to page five and my heart sank. I thought that I'd included a chart detailing the specifics of the sales boost. It wasn't there.

"My mistake," I said. I quickly tried to remedy the situation by explaining it and apologizing again. I managed to smooth it over, but my father's eyes told me another story. He was clearly pissed off. When the meeting was over, he told me to stick around because he wanted to talk to me.

"What the hell was that?" My father had just closed the door. His deep voice filled up the entire office. "I treat you the same way I treat any other employee, regardless of whether you're my son or not. I expect you to be prepared."

My father knew how to make me feel like a kid all over again. I knew I'd fucked up. I allowed my thoughts of Remi to cloud my mind and it had fucked up the presentation. Professionally speaking, I didn't really make too many mistakes, so it wasn't like he had to clean up too many of my messes like Brandon.

"I apologize," I said simply. "It won't

happen again." I looked him in the eye so he knew how serious I was.

"Please make sure it doesn't," he said. He turned and headed towards the door. "I don't know where your mind was but you need to get it straight. I love you. See you later." With that, he turned and headed out the door without waiting for a response.

I sent Remi a text letting her know what time and where we could meet for dinner. I'd chosen a restaurant that was outside the normal places I went. I wasn't trying to get caught by Chloe or anyone that she knew. I usually picked women up for dates but I wasn't trying to be spotted anywhere near where Remi lived. There was a certain level of danger involved in all of this and it made it that much more exciting.

I headed back to my place after work to change. I'd finally managed to talk to Chloe and she sounded a lot better than she was the night before. I told her that I'd see her later on because I was having dinner with my parents. She understood, which made it easier for me.

The restaurant we were going to later was kind of fancy. I put on a pair of light blue jeans, a white button down shirt and my long trench coat. It was supposed to be kind of chilly.

I got to the restaurant a few minutes before 8 and checked my car in with the valet. At 8 on the dot Remi arrived. She stepped out of her car in what seemed like slow motion. She got out and I had to do a double-take. She looked amazing.

Her long hair was curled at the sides and she had on red lipstick and no makeup. She was wearing a midnight blue dress that was short but still classy. It showed off her legs and all of her curves. Damn, she looked good. All of the second guessing I'd been doing was gone.

I walked up to her and greeted her. She handed her keys to the valet and walked over to me. I leaned down and greeted her with a kiss on the cheek.

"Wassup?" I smiled at her and looked her up and down. She seemed to be as impressed with me because she was nodding at me with approval.

"How are you?" She smiled back. "So I see that you can dress. Third time I've seen you and you look great each time."

"Thanks," I said. "So do you. You ready to head inside?"

"Sure," she said.

We headed inside and I told the hostess my name. She escorted us to a table in the back. I'd specifically requested somewhere private. I wanted to make sure that we wouldn't be spotted. I ordered a bottle of red wine. The waiter came and brought it over to us and poured out two glasses.

Remi and I hadn't really said much to one another. It was clear that we were both nervous about all of this. After a couple of sips of wine, I decided to break the ice.

"This is awkward," I said. I glanced up from my glass of wine and looked into her eyes. "It doesn't have to be though."

"What makes you say that?"

"Well, it's clear there's something between us," I said. "And I think it's best to just explore it now since we're both here. Besides, it's not like we can go back and take away from what we did the other night."

"I mean, we could have just left it there and not spoken again," Remi said. "But neither of us wanted to do that, so here we are."

"True," I said. I got quiet again. "So how about this? How about we just enjoy the date like it's any other date. We don't have to mention Chloe unless she comes up in the conversation, but we can just spend time getting to know one another."

"Sounds good," Remi smiled at me. "So tell me more about you. I don't need to know about Kaiden Briggs the big-time CEO's son and all that. Tell me who you are as a person besides all that."

I smiled at her again. "Cool, no problem. Well, I'm a hard worker. We were well off when I was young and got richer over time, but my father made sure that stayed grounded. He and my mother wanted us to know how to work hard."

"How many siblings do you have? I met your brother at the club with you. Is it just the two of you?"

"Nah, we have a baby sister too," I said. "Well, not a baby cause she's grown. What about you?"

"That's cool," Remi said. "And no siblings for me. I don't know if I mentioned it before, but I was adopted. My parents couldn't have kids naturally so they adopted me. They made it clear that they loved me and I loved them too. I never wanted to go look for my birth parents because I had everything I needed growing up. When they died, it hurt but it made me stronger too."

"That's good," I said to her. "So how was your day?"

"It was great. I'm working on a new clothing line. I'm trying to expand what I've been doing. I'll be looking for models for a show soon enough. It's really exciting."

"I'm happy you're so passionate about your work. I meet too many people nowadays who only wanna do shit for money and it ends up failing because there's no passion behind it," I said.

"That's true," she responded. "What about you? How was your day?"

I took another sip of the wine. "It was cool. I did mess up on a big presentation earlier though."

"Why?"

"Well, I'm always prepared and stuff but I was nervous all day. I had other things on my mind," I explained.

"Like what?" she asked.

"You," I said with a smirk. "All day long I was thinking about you and this date. I was second guessing myself but I'm glad I'm here with you."

"Me too," she said. "I was thinking about it all day. I was going to text you to cancel it and whenever my phone went off I thought it was you trying to cancel it." She laughed. "I'm also glad I came."

Remi and I had a lot more in common than I'd originally thought. She was like me in so many ways. We laughed and joked like we'd known each other for a while. We went through the whole bottle of wine and got another one. Before we knew what was happening it was almost one in the morning.

"I didn't realize it was so late. I'm gonna be exhausted at work tomorrow," Remi said.

"Me too," I said. "It was worth it though." The waiter came back over and handed me back my credit card. We got up and headed outside and handed our keys to the valets. I had to admit that after going through two bottles of wine, I was feeling a little buzzed. Remi was standing in front of me and I was eyeing her from behind. I was imagining what it would be like to just go back to her place with her and take my time and slowly show her how good of a lover I could be. I had to resist.

Instead, I did the smart thing. Our cars came out around the same time and I gave her a kiss on the cheek and let her know I'd be speaking to her soon enough.

"I'll be looking forward to it," Remi said. I stood there and watched her get in her car and drive away. I was tempted to follow her but decided to just head over to Chloe's house instead.

I got to Chloe's house soon enough and she was sleep. I took off my clothes and climbed into bed. I kissed her on the cheek. She was clearly still mad at me because of what happened before. She rolled over and stayed on her side of the bed. I was feeling guilty as hell but I pushed it from my mind. I didn't know where things with Remi and I were going and I decided not to spend too much time thinking about it either. I closed my eyes and fell asleep.

CHAPTER 9

Remi

I WALKED into the office a little later than usual. Karla was already there sitting at her desk. When I walked in she greeted me and I had to stifle a yawn before I greeted her.

Kaiden and I had been out so late the night before. Going into the date with him, I really had no idea of what to expect. I knew that we were in dangerous territory. I wanted to go but like I'd told him the night before, I was hoping one of us would have the balls to cancel.

Kaiden was different from people that I'd dated previously. I wasn't trying to get it all in my head that we were a couple or anything because clearly, he was committed to my Aunt Chloe, but it was nice to at least enjoy him for the night. Kaiden was attentive and knew when to listen, but could also keep a conversation going. We talked about everything under the sun almost nonstop. It was probably one of the best dates that I'd ever been on.

I sat behind my desk and started answering and sending emails. I also went ahead and pulled out my sketch book. I had a program on my computer that could replace the sketch pad but there was something about using an actual pencil and paper to make my designs that made them more real.

As much as I wanted to focus on my designs, I couldn't. Kaiden and the thought of him in his suit...and out of his suit came to my mind. I was hoping last night that he wanted to come back to my place or something and for a moment I thought he wanted to but nothing happened. I really wanted the chance to have sex with him again without having to rush through it like last time. His body was amazing. He also knew how to use his d—

"Remi!" Karla's loud voice snapped me

from my thoughts. I looked up and saw her staring at me.

"What? Why you yelling?" I leaned back in my chair.

"'Cause I been calling you for damn near a whole minute and you ain't answering. Then you started blushing and shit. I thought you were sick or something," Karla explained.

"No. No, I'm fine," I said. I was sick though...lovesick for Kaiden Briggs. I had it bad.

"Hmm," she said while she eyed me suspiciously. "Something's up. What got you all hot and bothered? Is it a man?"

I shook my head. Karla could be so damn nosey. "No," I said, trying to throw her off my scent. I picked up my pencil and tried to start drawing again.

"Nope!" Karla said loudly. 'You lying! It is a man. Spill the beans, girl." She was smiling at me now with a big cheesy grin. I guess I couldn't hide from her.

"You so nosey," I said sucking my teeth playfully. "Yeah it is a man."

"Who is he? Do I know him?" Karla moved over to my desk and sat in front of it. She put her elbows up on the desk and put her hands in her face. She was all ears.

"No you don't know him," I said. "You did see him though. You remember Kaiden from the other night at the club?"

She nodded. "Yeah, him and his fine ass brother," I said. "I should text him."

"Well, the other night I went to Aunt Chloe's gala and he was there. One thing led to another and we ended up having sex behind one of the curtains," I said.

Karla's eyes got all wide and she busted out in another big grin. "Yessssssss," she said. She threw her hands in the air like she'd just won the lottery. "Your drought is over! Look at you getting some, and behind a curtain at that? That's one of my moves. I'm happy for you."

"Thanks," I said. I knew her opinion would probably change once she heard the rest of it. "So last night he and I went on a date." I said it flatly, trying to think about it all and feeling a little bit of guilt.

"Why you sound so depressed about it? Was it a good date?" Karla looked concerned.

"No, it was amazing. We went to this Italian

place and talked for hours. It was probably one of the best dates I've ever been on," I explained.

"So what's the problem?" Karla asked.

"He has a girlfriend," I said dramatically.

Karla rolled her eyes. "Oh, girl, please," she said as she waved her hand dismissively. "You know my rules when it comes to stuff like that. The person who has to respect the relationship is the person who is in the relationship. If he's taking you out on dates and what not, what does it say about him and whoever he's with? Besides, you don't know the girlfriend and she ain't gonna find out so don't trip."

I looked up and looked her in the eyes so she knew I was serious. "I do know the girlfriend," I said. I paused and took a deep breath before I went on. "It's my Aunt Chloe."

Karla didn't say anything. Her eyes got all wide and she looked at me trying to see if I was joking or not. She then started smiling.

"What's so funny?" I snapped.

"Girl this is just a crazy situation," she said. "Only you or me would get into some shit like that."

"I know," I said. "But what am I supposed to

do? I need your advice. I'm really stuck between a rock and a hard place."

"How do you feel about him?" Karla asked.

"I really like him," I said. "I know it's fucked up but I do. I also know it's only been a few days but it just seems like there's so much potential there. I really want to see where this could go. Like he's handsome, charming, and everything else I look for in a man. He'd be perfect if he wasn't—"

"If he wasn't fucking your aunt's ass," Karla interrupted. I looked at her and rolled my eyes.

"Yes," I said.

"Well look," Karla began, "I know I usually support all the craziness you can get into and you do the same for me, but this situation is obviously different. Your aunt raised you after your parents died and is like another mom to you. You don't want to fuck up her relationship."

"I know, but you know how Chloe is," I said. I know I asked her for advice but I really wanted her to see my point of view. "She be running through guys like it's going out of style. You know she always has a new man that has to be at least 10 years younger than her at a minimum. Her and Kaiden been messing around for a few months and his time is gonna be up soon enough. If there's anything I know about my aunt it's that she can't keep a man. So I figure that if he and I date behind her back then a few months after they break up, we won't have to."

Karla didn't say anything. She sat back, clearly in thought. I really needed her opinion because I was really at a loss for what I should do. So many thoughts were running through my mind. If there was something between Kaiden and I, didn't I have the right to explore it? On the other hand, I knew I was wrong for essentially screwing over my Aunt Chloe in the pursuit of what I wanted.

"Girl look," Karla said, snapping me from my thoughts, "you're not the type to just randomly chase after dudes. It's clear that you like him and you owe it to yourself to see where it goes. I know he's with your Aunt but like you said, she just runs through guys like him. Follow your heart. That's the best advice I can give you. If you're meant to be with Kaiden, it'll happen," she finished.

"Thanks so much!" I got up and walked

around the desk and hugged her. "I really appreciate it."

"No problem," Karla said. "But if this blows up in your face, don't blame me," she added with a laugh, half serious and half joking.

"I know, right?" I said, taking my seat. "Now I'm just gonna relax and wait for him to call me like he said he would."

Since I'd finally been able to get that out of my mind and off of my chest, I was a lot more productive at work. I managed to get through several designs and had some new styling clients lined up. I hadn't heard from Kaiden all day, but it was cool. He, like me, was a career person so I knew he was probably busy at work.

After work I was in my car driving home and my phone went off. I was at a stoplight so I answered.

Hey, the text from Kaiden read. *What are you up to?*

I quickly typed out my reply. *Heading home. You?*

At work still. I was thinking we should talk.

I had to admit that I was hype. I really wanted to hear from him and it was great that he reached out to me. I knew I was acting like a happy school girl but I really wanted to see him again. Kaiden and I were really connected and I knew he had to be feeling it too.

Ok cool. Come over later on and we can talk, read the text I sent. He told me alright.

When I got home I decided that I needed to pick something to wear. I was hype as hell that I'd be seeing him later on that night and I knew he would be too.

I knew it might have been a little bit foolish, but I was sure that when Kaiden came over later, he and I would talk about our future and he'd tell me he was leaving Chloe. I wasn't trying to imagine a life with Kaiden or anything. I just wanted to make sure that whatever was happening between us had the right amount of time to blossom into whatever it was going to be.

As I thumbed through my closet, I couldn't help but think about what would happen as far as my relationship with Aunt Chloe was concerned. I was sure that if things between Kaiden and I progressed then we'd have to tell Chloe about it. Knowing her, I was sure that she'd be a little pissed off, but Chloe was older and mature. She knew the risks when it came to being in a relationship. I wasn't trying to be fucked up, but I wished that she'd give us her blessing if we did end up together.

Most of all I was excited that I was feeling romantic again. Since Jackson and I broke up, I'd been feeling a lot less romantic, but Kaiden had woken up all of those feelings inside of me again. I was glad that I'd been lucky to find one of the good ones.

CHAPTER 10

Kaiden

TODAY HAD BEEN a day at work. I'd finally managed to close some accounts that the company had been after for a while. I also had lunch with Brandon where he told me about some new chick he was smashing. I listened to it halfheartedly, trying to focus on him, but I couldn't.

The guilt that I thought I'd pushed away the other night had finally come back and hit me full force. At first I tried not to let it all get to me, but after a while I couldn't fight it. I was beating myself up.

Since my date with Remi, I'd had a little

time to think and I was finally able to come to a conclusion. What Chloe and I had wasn't perfect, but it was a good thing. I didn't know what the future held for she and I but I always tried to be a man of my word, and I'd told Chloe when we first started dating that I'd never purposely hurt her. I'd already done that by sleeping with and going on a date with Remi behind her back, but I wasn't trying to take it any further than that.

I felt like I'd ruined a good thing by going on the date with Remi. Chloe had her ways but she'd never given me a reason not to trust her or to disrespect her.

The problem was that no matter how much I wanted to remain true to my feelings and things, I almost felt like I owed it to myself to see where things could go between Remi and I. Remi had it going on. She seemed to be perfect for me, and if I'd met her before I met Chloe, there would be no issue about which way I'd go. The shit with Remi was exciting and new but Chloe had been the same way once. It was fucked up that Chloe and I had this big ass issue going on but I couldn't even tell her about it. I'd put myself into this position and because of that, I was the only one who could get myself out.

Before I left work, I sent Remi a text letting her know that we should talk. I wanted to let her know how I felt and explain to her that even though things between us seemed good, we couldn't get with one another. It would be difficult to do but it was the right thing.

After work, I decided to head to Chloe's house. I wanted to talk to her about how things had been going between us. I didn't plan on telling her about what happened with Remi though. I didn't need for more than one relationship to be destroyed by our mistake.

As I walked into Chloe's house I got a text from Remi. She was asking me if we were still on for later. I sighed and thought about responding but decided not to.

I walked over to Chloe's liquor cabinet and opened it, grabbed a bottle of whiskey and a glass and poured some out. I looked at the brown liquor in the glass for a moment before I drank it all down in one gulp and poured out another one.

Either way someone was going to get hurt, and I think that was the most difficult part for me. I didn't mind being the bad guy but there were so many ways that this could go. The more that I thought about it, the more I realized what was for the best. Chloe was my girlfriend, not Remi. I had to think of her and her feelings first.

I was anxious as I waited for Chloe to get home. I'd stopped at the florist and picked out a dozen long stem roses for her. She probably would think I was trying to make up for the other night when we didn't have sex, and I wasn't going to make her think anything other than that.

After a while longer, I heard Chloe's car pull up outside. I headed outside to her car and opened the door for her. She took one look at me and rolled her eyes. She grabbed her purse and stepped out of the car, making sure to not be anywhere close to me.

"Chloe...," I said in a pleading way. I handed her the flowers. They brushed up against her suit jacket as she marched on towards her front door. "Chloe!" I said it a little louder. It was clear that she was trying her hardest to ignore me. I couldn't blame her. I usually never turned her down for sex, and my excuse was weak. I knew that much to be true.

She got to her front door and opened it. She was closing it in my face and trying to leave me outside. I had a key and I could have used it to open the door, but I wanted her to let me in.

"Please, just don't close the door," I said. "We need to talk." I tried again to hand her the flowers but she wasn't having it.

"You think some flowers and shit are gonna solve this?" she snapped at me and finally stopped trying to close the door. "You can't fix everything with gifts! I can buy my own shit, in case you forgot," she said.

"I know," I said. "Can you give me a chance to explain?"

She stood in the doorway not saying anything. She sucked her teeth and rolled her eyes but didn't say anything else. Chloe stepped to the side and let me into the house. We walked silently to the living room. I tried again to hand her the flowers but she wouldn't take them. I just sat them on the counter as we passed the kitchen.

We sat down on her couch on opposite sides. She turned her body to face me and the look on her face told me all I needed to know. She was pissed off and wasn't about to let me off that easily.

"Now look," Chloe said. "I don't know what's been going on with you, but for the last few days you been acting funny and then when you didn't want to have sex with me, it hurt me and pissed me off. You've been acting strange and I think I deserve an explanation."

"You do," I said. "You do." I paused and took a deep breath. The first thought that came to my mind was that I should just tell Chloe the truth. She'd be upset and be hurt but in the long run she'd be able to deal with the truth more than some lies that I could spill to her.

The problem was that I'd always had a problem when it came to women; I hated hurting them. I could run through as much as I wanted but I was always honest with them. No matter what I wanted from them—relationships, business partnerships, sex—I always tried to remain up front with them. I never fucked a girl and moved on without telling her from the beginning that's what I planned on doing. I couldn't find the confidence to come clean and hurt Chloe. I thought that I could but it wasn't really an option for me. The best thing to do would be for me to just go and forget about Remi and what happened between us.

I had to lie and that wasn't hard for me to do. I knew it was fucked up and what I was about to do was even more fucked up but it had to be done.

"This has to do with Remi," I said.

Chloe's face screwed up and she looked like she wanted to flip but didn't say anything for a little bit. "What does this have to do with her?"

"I know I been acting strange and shit and it's all for a reason. It has to do with Remi." I paused and took a deep breath. I was about to tell a huge lie and I needed to be composed for it. "I had to ask Remi something...something important..."

Remi

The sounds of Maxwell's This Woman's Work sounded through the speakers in my apartment. I was setting the mood. I'd just gotten out the shower and I was still kind of damn damn as I applied coconut oil to my skin. I wanted to make sure that I was all silky and smooth for when Kaiden arrived. I'd asked him earlier if he was still coming but he hadn't responded. I decided to get ready just in case.

I had a lot of lingerie from when Jackson and I were together. I thumbed through it, trying to find the perfect thing to put on. I finally decided to keep it simple. I had a black lace one piece that pushed up my cleavage and showed off my thick thighs and fat ass. I wanted it all to be on display for when Kaiden came.

I headed into the living room and lit some scented candles. I knew I was doing a lot but I was trying to set the mood. I wanted to make sure he understood it was a romantic night. I put on my silk robe and waited.

Right on time there was a knock at the door. "Showtime," I smiled to myself. Kaiden was right on time and it was time for him and I to get down to business.

I opened the door and was shocked. Kaiden was standing there but in front of him was Aunt Chloe. I closed my robe and pulled myself together a little bit.

"Aunt Chloe? Kaiden? What are you two

doing here?" I asked. I was surprised. I hoped he hadn't told her about what we did. She didn't look pissed off though, so who knew what it was about.

"I had to tell you the news!" Chloe burst out into this cheesy grin. She held up her left hand where she showed off a huge diamond ring. "Kaiden proposed and I said yes!"

"Oh, my God," I said. Shock was written all over my face, but not for the right reason. Chloe grabbed me and pulled me into her, gripping me tightly in a hug. I eyed Kaiden from behind her back. I tried to look him in the eyes but he was staring at the floor like a little kid who'd been caught in the cookie jar.

Find out what happens next in part two of What She Don't Know! Available Now!

To find out when Mia Black has new books available, **follow Mia Black on Instagram: @authormiablack**

WHAT SHE DON'T KNOW 2

Remi knew better than to cross that line, but now things have gone too far. Her aunt has given her everything and more. She's not so sure she's ready to take anything away from her, even if that means she has to live with the pain of losing Kaiden.

Will they do the right thing and stay clear of each other or will their undeniable attraction keep pulling them closer and closer together?

Find out what happens next in part two of What She Don't Know! Available Now!

Follow Mia Black on Instagram for more updates: @authormiablack

Made in the USA
Lexington, KY
22 June 2019